*Tilly, Tom and Tiny and*
# The Never-Ending Magic Rain Adventure

Written by Andrew Davenport
*Illustrated by Joan and Jane Hickson*

**Hippo**

Scholastic Children's Books,
7-9 Pratt Street, London NW1 0AE

A division of Scholastic Publications Ltd
London – New York – Toronto – Sydney – Auckland

Published by Scholastic Publications Ltd 1995
Text copyright © Ragdoll Productions (UK) Ltd 1995
Illustrations copyright © Joan and Jane Hickson 1995

Design of Tots-TV puppets and house
copyright © Ragdoll Productions (UK) Ltd 1993
Central logo copyright © Central independent Television plc 1989
Based on the Central Independent Television series
produced by Ragdoll Productions

ISBN: 0 590 13253 9

Typeset by Rapid Reprographics
Printed and bound in Hong Kong

10 9 8 7 6 5 4 3 2 1

Right in the middle of a wood, where
nobody thinks of looking, where the
bracken grows high, and the trees
grow close together, there's a little
yellow house.

It's not very big,
it's not very new,
But this house is magic.

This is the house where Tilly, Tom and
Tiny live with their friend Donkey.

(Naughty Furryboo lives there too, but
that's a secret.)

They all live together in their magic
secret house,
and nobody sees,
and nobody knows.

Tilly is the most magical Tot.

She has a magic flute which she
keeps on a ribbon round her neck.

Every morning she goes into the
woods, finds a place to sit, and plays
magical music.

And when she plays, it is almost as if
her music makes the whole wood
grow a little more green, and a little
more still, and a little more alive.

One morning, when Tilly was out in the woods, Tiny was looking for small animals with his binoculars.

On the path by the front step, he found a trail of ants. And under a leaf in the flowerbed, there was a snail.

In the corner of the doorframe, a spider had made a web, and under a flat stone in a damp corner by the wall, there was a little worm.

"That's my favourite one of all!" said Tiny.

Then he looked around for something else.

Over by the oak tree was a big green bottom. It was Tom bending over, digging a hole. Tiny went to see what he was doing.

"Hello Tom!" said Tiny.

"Hello Tiny!" said Tom. "Look – I've got a secret!"

Tom carefully took something out of his pocket, and showed it to Tiny. It was a little black speck, no bigger than a grain of sugar.

"What's that?" said Tiny in a whisper.

"It's a seed!" said Tom. "I'm going to plant it in this hole."

"What for?" said Tiny, who didn't know about seeds.

"So that it will grow into a great big flower!"

"Cor Tom!" said Tiny. "Is that little teeny insy winsy titchy witchy seed really going to grow into a great big lovely flower?"

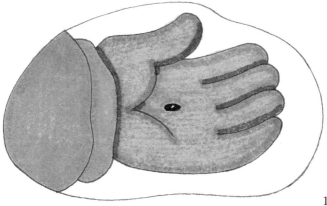

"Yes!" said Tom, and he gave the
seed a little kiss, put it in the hole,
and gently covered it over with earth.
"There we are little seed – all nice
and comfy in the ground," he said.

Tiny looked at the little patch of earth through his binoculars.

"It's not growing yet Tom," he said.

"Tiny, Tiny!" said Tom. "Seeds take a very very long long time to grow!"

13

Just then, Tilly came by, on her way back from the woods.

"Bonjour Tom! Bonjour Tiny!" she said.

Tom told her all about the seed he had planted.

"It's going to take a very very long long time to grow!" said Tiny.

"Ooh la la la la!" said Tilly.

Then Tiny had an idea.

"Maybe Tilly could play a magic tune to the seed, to help it grow a little bit faster."

Tilly thought this was a good idea, so the Tots all sat down, and she started to play.

It was very magical music indeed. Tom and Tiny listened, and waited. And then something happened.

Plip! A big wet raindrop landed on Tiny's head.

Plop! A big wet raindrop landed on Tom's head.

Ploop! A big wet raindrop landed right on Tilly's nose.

"Oh no!" said Tom. "It's starting to rain!"

And the Tots jumped up, ran into the house, and closed all the windows and shut all the doors.

And only just in time.

Flash! went the lightning. Crash! went the thunder, and down came all the rain.

It rained, and it rained, and it rained.

It splashed on the path, and rattled on the roof, it gushed in the gutters, and drummed on the doors, and it tappled all over the windows.

But inside their magic secret house, the Tots were warm and dry.

"Cor!" said Tom, "I think Tilly must have played a magic extra-rain tune!"
"Ooh la la! Oui!" said Tilly, a little bit surprised.

Tiny sat in the window, looking out.
"I'm glad we're indoors," he said, and he wondered about all the small animals in the garden.

Outside, the clouds rolled and rumbled across the sky, and the rain fell for the whole afternoon.

It got so dark that Tom had to put the light on, even though it was daytime.

At teatime, they filled up the bucket
with carrots, and Tom put up his
umbrella and took them to Donkey in
his shed.

When he got back, he said it was the wettest, rainiest rain ever.

"You're wet all over!" said Tiny.
It was still raining when the Tots went to bed.

It was still raining in the middle of the night, when Tiny got up to look out of the window.

And it was still raining when the Tots woke up in the morning.

"This is never-ending rain!" said Tiny.

"Oh dear!" said Tom, as he set off with Donkey's breakfast, "I hope it doesn't rain for ever."

But this time, when he got back, Tom said he thought the rain wasn't quite as rainy as it was before, and the sky was a little bit brighter.

Tiny noticed that there wasn't so much rain running down the window, and Tilly picked up her flute for the first time since the rain began, and played a getting-brighter tune.

Then, just before lunchtime, Tom
noticed a funny sort of quietness.

"It's coming from the garden," he
thought, and he opened the front
door, and looked out.

"Tilly! Tiny!" he called back into the
house, "I don't think it's raining any
more!"

Tilly ran down the stairs. Tiny rushed
to put his shoes on.

Outside, the air was fresh and light, and everything felt all wet and clean.

Tilly sat down on the cart, and began to play magical after-the-rain music.

One by one, the birds began chirping and fluttering in the trees.

Donkey came along the path, took a
big mouthful of lush green grass and
chewed on it happily, looking all
around.

And then the sun began to shine.

Tiny noticed that a snail had ventured out onto the wet path, the ants had started milling about on the windowsill, and that a spider was peeping out of a crack in the doorframe.

"All the small animals were safe in the rain!" he said.

Then he lifted up the flat stone by the
wall. Underneath, the iggly wiggly
worm was busily feeling around in
the mud with its pointy nose.

"That's my favourite one of all,"
said Tiny.

But then Tom called out.

"Tilly! Tiny! Come and see!"

Tom was pointing at the place where
he had planted his seed.

A little green shoot was just
beginning to show above the earth.

"It's my little tiny seed!" said Tom.

"It's started to grow already!"

"So Tilly's music did work!" said
Tiny.

"It made the magic rain, specially
to help it grow!" said Tom.

And they gave Tilly one big kiss each.

"Clever Tilly!" they said.

And they went off together to play in the sunshine.

So, if ever you're out in the woods, and one minute it's sunny and the next minute it's raining, somebody's probably playing magic growing music.

And you might not be very far from the magic secret house where Tilly, Tom and Tiny live.

But remember –

it's a secret!